D0170958

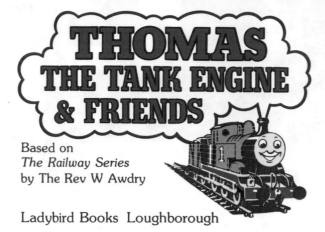

THOMAS THE TANK ENGINE & FRIENDS

Based on
The Railway Series
by The Rev W Awdry

Ladybird Books Loughborough

Acknowledgment
Photographic stills by Kenny McArthur of Clearwater Features
for Britt Allcroft Ltd.

British Library Cataloguing in Publication Data
Awdry, W.
    Thomas & Terence; James & the tar wagons.—
    (Thomas the tank engine & friends; 3)
    I. Title   II. McArthur, Kenny
    III. Awdry, W. James & the tar wagons   IV. Series
    823'.914[J]   PZ7
    ISBN 0-7214-0894-X

THOMAS AND
TERENCE

Thomas and Terence

Autumn had come to the Island of
Sodor. The leaves were changing from
green to brown. The fields were changing
too, from yellow stubble to brown earth.

As Thomas puffed along on his branch
line with Annie and Clarabel, he heard

the "chug chug chug" of a tractor at work.

One day, stopping for a signal, he saw the tractor close by. "Hullo!" said the tractor. "I'm Terence; I'm ploughing."

"Hullo!" said Thomas. "I'm Thomas; I'm pulling a train. What *ugly* wheels you've got."

Terence said that his wheels were not ugly. "They're caterpillars!" he said. "I can go anywhere; *I* don't need rails."

At the other end of the tunnel he
could see that a heap of snow had fallen
from the sides of the cutting.

"Silly soft stuff!" said Thomas and he charged into the snow. "Cinders and ashes!" he cried. "I'm stuck!" – and he was.

"Back, Thomas, back!" called his driver. Thomas tried to go back but his wheels spun round and he couldn't move. More snow fell down and piled up around him.

The guard went back for help while the driver, fireman and passengers tried to dig the snow away from Thomas's wheels. But as fast as they dug, more snow slipped down and Thomas was nearly buried.

"Oh! My wheels and coupling rods!" said Thomas. "I shall have to stop here until I'm frozen. What a silly engine I am." And Thomas began to cry.

At last a bus came to rescue all the
passengers. Then Terence the tractor
came chugging through the tunnel. Snow
never worried him. He pulled the empty
coaches away and came back for
Thomas.

Thomas's wheels were clear but they
still spun round and round when he tried
to move. Terence tugged and slipped,
and slipped and tugged.

At last he pulled Thomas clear of the snow, ready for the journey home.

"Thank you, Terence, your caterpillars are *splendid*," said Thomas, gratefully.

"I hope that you will be sensible now, Thomas," said his driver, crossly.

"I'll try," said Thomas, as he puffed home.

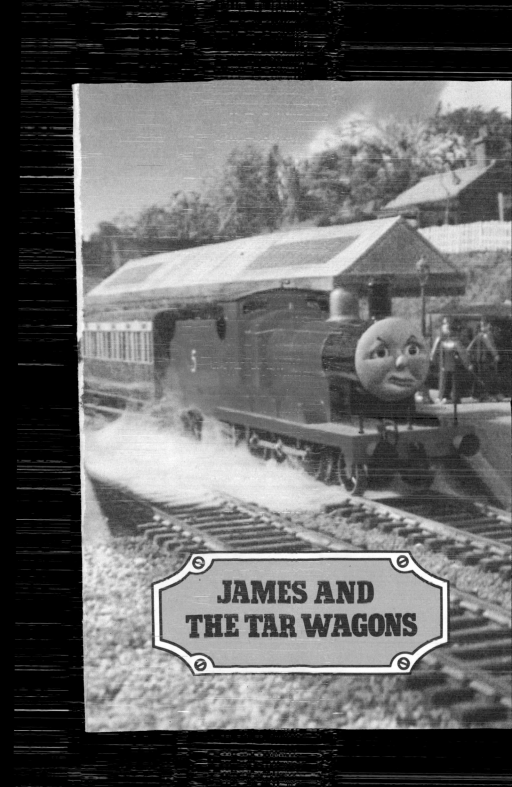

JAMES AND
THE TAR WAGONS

James and the tar wagons

Toby is a tram engine. He is short and sturdy and has a coach called Henrietta. They enjoy their job on the Island of Sodor.

Every morning they take the workmen to the quarry and they often meet James at the junction.

Toby and Henrietta look very old-fashioned. They were shabby and needed new paint when they first came and James was rude whenever he saw them.

"Ugh! What dirty objects!" he would say as they passed by.

One day Toby lost patience. "James," he said, "why are you red?"

"I am a splendid engine," replied James, loftily. "I am ready for anything. You never see *my* paint dirty."

"Oh," said Toby, innocently, "that's why you once needed bootlaces – to be ready, I suppose!"

James felt redder than ever and snorted off. It was such an insult to be reminded of the time when a passenger's bootlace had been used to mend a hole in one of his coaches. And all because he had gone too fast.

At the end of the line James left his
coaches and got ready for his next train.
It was a 'slow goods', stopping at every
station to pick up and set down trucks.
James hated slow goods trains.

"Dirty trucks from dirty sidings!" he
grumbled.

Starting with only a few, James picked up more and more trucks until he had a long train.

At first, the trucks behaved well but James bumped them so crossly that they soon decided to pay him back.

They went over the viaduct and it wasn't long before they reached the top of Gordon's hill. Heavy goods trains should wait there so that the guard can 'pin down' their brakes. This stops the trucks pushing the engines too fast as they go down the hill.

James had had an accident with trucks once before on Gordon's hill. He should have remembered this.

"Wait, James, wait!" said his driver, but James did not wait. He was too busy thinking about what he would say to Toby when they next met.

"Hurrah! Hurrah!" laughed the trucks. They banged their buffers and pushed James down the hill. The guard tightened his brakes.

"On! On! On!" cried the trucks.

"I've *got* to stop. I've *got* to stop," groaned James.

They thundered through the station and lurched into the yard.

There was a crash and something
sticky splashed all over James.

He had run into two tar wagons and
was black from smoke-box to cab. He

was more dirty than hurt but the wagons
and some trucks were broken to pieces.
The breakdown train was in the yard and
they soon tidied up the mess.

Toby and Percy were sent to help and came as quickly as they could.

"Look there, Percy!" said Toby. "Whatever is that dirty object?"

"That's James," replied Percy. "Didn't you know?"

"Well, it's James's shape," said Toby, "but James is a splendid *red* engine and you never see *his* paint dirty."

James pretended that he hadn't heard.

Toby and Percy cleared away the
unhurt trucks and helped James home.

The Fat Controller came to meet them.
"Well done, Percy and Toby!" he said,
smiling.

He turned to James. "Fancy letting
your trucks run away. I *am* surprised!
You're not fit to be seen; you must be
cleaned at once," he said.

"Toby shall have a new coat of paint – chocolate and blue, I think," said the Fat Controller.

"Please, sir, can Henrietta have one too?" asked Toby.

"Certainly, Toby," said the Fat Controller. "She shall have brown, like Annie and Clarabel, Thomas's coaches."

Toby smiled. He knew that Henrietta would be delighted and he ran off happily to tell her the good news.